L. Shefren

J. Mayfield

What Kind Of Family Do You Have?

What Kind Of Family Do You Have?

Gretchen Super
Illustrated by Kees de Kiefte

Troll Associates

To my family—the place where I belong

GS

For Daphne, Caspar, and Oskar

KDK

Library of Congress Cataloging in Publication Data

Super, Gretchen
What Kind Of Family Do You Have?
Illustrated by Kees de Kiefte

Includes index.
Summary: Examines different kinds of families, including a nuclear
family, extended family, and adoptive family, and describes the
interpersonal relationships that make them function.
1. Family—Juvenile literature. [1. Family. 2. Family life.]
I. Kiefte, Kees de, ill. II. Title. III. Series: Your Family Album.
HQ518.S843   1991   306.85—dc20   90-24381   CIP   AC

Text Copyright © 1991
Twenty-First Century Books

Illustrations Copyright © 1991
Kees de Kiefte

Printed in the United States of America

10 9 8 7 6 5 4 3 2 1

Table of Contents

Different Kinds Of Families

Do you remember the day of your
class picture?
Did you comb your hair
to look your best?
Did you have to say "Cheeseburger"—
and smile?
It was hard not to laugh.

Take a look at your class picture.
Look at all the kids.
You know kids who are different
in so many ways.
There are kids who look different.
And kids who like to do different things.
And you know kids who live
in different kinds of families.

This book is about many kinds
of families.
They may be like your family
in some ways.
They may be unlike your family
in other ways.

Every family is a different group
of people.
And families are as different as the
people who live in them.

Let's meet some different families.

A Nuclear Family

Rachel lives with her mom and dad
and her little brother, Jake.
Soon there will be a new baby
in the family, too.
Rachel lives in a nuclear family.
A mother, father, and their children
live in a nuclear family.

At Rachel's house, everybody has a
job to do.
Her mother even put a "Job Chart"
on the refrigerator door.
"You can't miss it," Rachel laughs.
Rachel's favorite job is feeding the cats.
"Here, Pickles," she shouts from the
porch. "Now where's Starshine?"

Rachel likes being the big sister.
She likes to play school with Jake.
"But why are *you* always the teacher?"
Jake asks.

They have fun for a while—until Jake
gets angry and walks away.
"Rachel is too bossy!" he cries.

Rachel's mom and dad both work.
So Rachel goes to a baby sitter
after school.
"I wish Grandma could be here
in the afternoon," Rachel says.
"Sometimes I wish I lived in a
bigger family."

Rachel sees her other relatives often.
On Sundays, Rachel's grandparents
may come to visit.
And it seems that every year there are
more cousins to play with.

Rachel likes it best of all when
Aunt Jackie spends the night.
Jackie paints Rachel's fingernails
and fixes her hair.
"Don't you look grown-up!"
Jackie says.

Rachel looks at herself
in the mirror.
"I wish you could
stay forever," she tells
her aunt.

But most times it's
mom and dad and
Rachel and Jake.
Rachel loves those
times, too.

Everyone is excited about the
new baby.
Rachel wonders whether it will be
a boy or girl.
"I'll have someone else to play with,"
she says.
"And someone else to boss around,"
Jake says.

Rachel likes living in her family.
It is the place where she belongs.

3

An Extended Family

José lives with his mom and dad and baby brother.

His uncle and grandmother also live with him.

José lives in an extended family.

Different relatives live together in an extended family.

It was hard for José when
his Uncle Ricky moved in.
The two of them had to share a
bedroom, and it was too crowded.

"What *is* all this junk?" Ricky asked.
There were piles of bottle caps and
rocks and even dead bugs.
José complained, "You're messing up
my collections!"

José kept tripping over his uncle's toolbox.

"Can't you put some of this stuff away?" José asked.

Ricky only said, "Those bugs are creepy."

José thought that he and his uncle would never get along.

"I wish he would go live somewhere else," José muttered.

After a while, José and Ricky got used to each other.

They still share a room, and it's still too crowded.

But it's not so messy anymore.

José made room in the closet for his uncle's tools.

And Ricky made a special wooden case for José's collections.

Sometimes José really enjoys sharing
his room.
"It's like having a big brother,"
he says.
And sometimes Ricky enjoys it, too.
But he still says, "That bug collection
gives me the creeps."

Once in a while, José wishes that he lived in a smaller family.
"This family is just too big," he says to himself.
It seems that there are too many people telling José what to do.
"And they all tell me different things!"

"But most of the time," José says, "it's just the right size."

It's just the right size when José needs
help with his homework.
It's the right size when everyone
crowds around the dinner table.
It's the right size when Grandma tells
her stories about the old days.
And it's just the right size whenever
José needs a friend to talk to.

José likes living in his family.
It is the place where he belongs.

An Adoptive Family

Peter lives with his mom and dad.
But they did not give birth to him.
Peter lives in an adoptive family.
In an adoptive family, the parents have
a child they did not give birth to.
The child becomes part of their family.

The man and woman who gave birth
to Peter are called his birth-parents.
Peter does not know who they are.

Peter's mother and father have told
him he is adopted.
They explained that his birth-parents
were not able to take care of a baby.
But his birth-parents loved Peter, and
they wanted him to have a good home.
They wanted him to live with people
who could take care of him.

Peter's parents wanted to have a baby.
But they were not able to have a child
of their own.
So they decided to adopt a child.
An adoption agency helped them find
a baby to raise as their own.
The agency helped them find Peter.

One time, Peter's best friend asked
him, "What is it like to be adopted?"
Peter didn't know what to say.
He was just a baby when he came
to live with his mom and dad.
They are the only family Peter has
ever known.

the day we brought
Peter home!

So Peter thought about his family.
How he and his mom walk Freddy,
their pet poodle.
"It's more like Freddy walks us," his
mom says.

How he loves to play checkers
with his dad.
Peter says, "Once in a while, I even
let him win."

Peter thought about all the things his
mom and dad do.

They check his homework.
They come to his soccer games.

They are so proud of him
when he does well in school.
They get annoyed with him
when he forgets to feed the dog.
And they love him all the time.

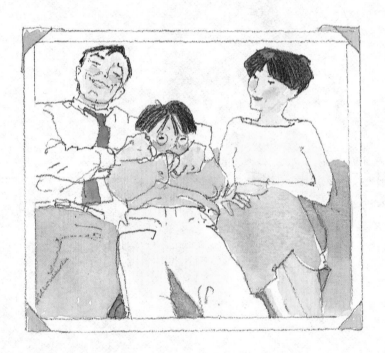

"I guess it's just like any other
family," Peter told his best friend.
"The only thing different is how you
get there. After that, it's all the same."

Now Peter's mom and dad are
waiting to adopt another baby.
The people from the adoption agency
came to visit Peter's family.
The agency had to be sure that they
would be good parents.
"They even asked *me* some questions,"
Peter says. "And I had to clean up
my room!"

The adoption agency decided that
Peter's family would make a good
home for a new baby.
The agency is trying to find a baby
for them, but it can take a long time.

Peter and his parents are getting ready
for the new baby.
They are fixing up the spare bedroom.
Peter even got out his old baby toys.

Peter hopes the baby will come soon.
"I can't wait to be a big brother,"
he says. "But will I have to keep my
room clean all the time?"

Peter likes living in his family.
It is the place where he belongs.

A Single-Parent Family

Carly lives with her mom.
Her big sister Marie lives with them
when she comes home from college.
Carly lives in a single-parent family.
Only one parent lives with the
children in a single-parent family.

Carly doesn't remember when her dad
lived with them.
He moved away when she was a baby.
Sometimes Carly wonders what it
would be like to have a father.
"Can you miss someone you never
knew?" she asks herself.

It's almost dinner time when Carly's
mom picks her up from day care.
Carly goes to day care after school
because her mom works.
It's a long day for Carly—and a long
day for her mom.

It was different before Marie left.
Carly would race home from school
to be with Marie.
It seemed that every day Marie taught
Carly something new.

She taught Carly how to catch a pop
fly and how to use the new computer.

"I miss you," Carly always writes
on her letters to Marie.
And her letters from Marie always
say, "I miss you back."

"Take good care of Puffin," Marie said
before she went away to college.
Puffin is Marie's cat, or at least he
used to be.
"Now Puffin thinks that he belongs to
me!" Carly says.

Each morning, he tickles her awake
with his whiskers.
Each night, he curls up and sleeps
at the foot of her bed.

Carly and her mom work together
to get dinner ready.

"I'm getting to be a pretty good
cook," Carly says proudly. "As long
as it's spaghetti and meatballs."

Carly helps her mom a lot.
They go grocery shopping and clean
the house together.

"Do I get paid for this?" Carly asks
with a laugh.

Her mother just smiles and says,
"Watch the meatballs, please."

Carly can't wait for the weekend.
Then her mom is not so rushed.
And the very best weekends are the
ones when Marie comes home.

Sometimes Carly and her mom visit
Marie at college.
Once, Carly even got to stay overnight
in Marie's room.

They stayed up late watching movies
and eating popcorn.
"I can't wait until I am old enough
to go to college," Carly says.

Most days are very busy for Carly
and her mom.
But sometimes they don't do much
of anything at all.
The time seems to go so slowly, and
Carly thinks maybe it will last forever.

Carly likes living in her family.
It is the place where she belongs.

A Blended Family

Tasha lives in two families.
She lives with her dad and her
stepfamily during the week.
And she lives with her mom
on the weekends.

Tasha explains it this way:
"My mom and dad got divorced.
After the divorce, my dad married
someone else.
She was divorced, too, and had a son
of her own."

Tasha's new family is called
a blended family.
In a blended family, people live together
who used to live in other families.
A blended family is also called
a stepfamily.
Tasha has a stepmother and stepbrother.

So now Tasha lives in two families.
Sometimes she gets tired of explaining
what kind of family she has.
"If *you* think it's confusing," Tasha
says, "think how *I* feel!"

It was very hard for Tasha when her
parents decided to get divorced.
She knew they were unhappy.
They used to argue most of the time.
The rest of the time, they hardly
spoke to each other.

But Tasha wanted her family
to stay together.
She hated it when her mom moved
to a new apartment.

When she was with her dad,
she missed her mom.
And when she was with her mom,
she missed her dad.

"I felt like I was split in two,"
Tasha says. "But there was only one
of me to go around."

It was even harder when her dad
decided to get married again.
Now she had two families.
Now she had two mothers.

"I don't need a new
mom," Tasha would
say. "I already have
one!"

But Tasha got used to living
in two families.
She really likes her stepmom.
They painted Tasha's bedroom together.
They made the ceiling look like a blue
sky filled with white, puffy clouds.
Tasha's stepbrother helped, too.
He made a sign that said "Tasha"
for her bedroom door.

Tasha likes to lie on her bed and look
up at the sky.
She knows that her mom and dad are
happy now.
She knows that they love her
as much as ever.

"Besides," she thinks, "it's kind of fun
to have two bedrooms."
She has a "weekend bedroom" at her
mom's apartment.
"Only now I have two bedrooms to
keep clean," Tasha adds.

Tasha spends part of each summer
with her mother, too.
They always go camping.
This summer, they are going to
the mountains.
"The tent is my third bedroom,"
Tasha laughs.

Tasha likes living in her two families.
They are the places where she belongs.

7

A Foster Family

Eric lives with his foster parents and
their two children.

Eric's parents are not able to take care
of him right now.

Eric lives in a foster family.

In a foster family, a new set of parents
takes care of a child for a while.

At first, Eric hated living
with his foster family.
He felt like he didn't belong
to this family.
"Why can't I just go home?" he asked.

But he knew he couldn't go home.
Eric knew that his parents were not
able to take care of him.

Eric doesn't like to talk about the
things that happened at home.
But it's hard for him not to think
about them.
His parents were treating him badly.
Sometimes they even forgot
that he was there.

There were many bad days at home.
But the worst day was when the
people from the social service agency
took him from his parents.
They said they were going to find a
foster home for him.
He would live there while his parents
tried to solve their problems.

"I didn't know what was going
to happen to me," he remembers.
"And I was scared."

For a long time, Eric was confused
about what happened.
Sometimes he blamed himself for his
parents' problems.

Sometimes he wondered whether they
didn't want him anymore.
"Maybe they just stopped loving me,"
he'd say.

Eric knows now that his mom and
dad still love him.
They visit him often and go with him
to a family counselor.
They are working hard to be
better parents.
And they hope Eric will be able to
come home soon.
"Me, too," Eric says.

And Eric really likes his foster family. They make him feel like a regular part of the family.

"I still miss my mom and dad," Eric says, "but my foster family is *all right!*"

Eric hopes he lives with his mom
and dad again soon.

But Eric likes living in his foster family.
For now, it is the place where he
belongs.

8

The Place Where
You Belong

Everyone you know lives in a family.

Every family is different.
Every family is a different group
of people.

But every family is the same, too.

A family is much more than just a
group of people.
It's where people love each other and
take care of each other.
It's where people share their lives
together.

What kind of family do you have?

There are all kinds of families.

But no matter what kind of family you have, your family is the place where you belong.

Words You Need To Know

There are many different kinds of families. "Your Family Album" will help you understand what a family is and what different families are like. Here are some words you should know:

adoption agency: a service that helps families adopt children

adoptive family: when parents have a child they did not give birth to

birth-parents: the man and woman who give birth to a child

blended family: when people live together who used to live in other families

conflict: when people in a family don't agree about their differences

divorce: when a husband and wife decide to end their marriage

extended family: when different relatives live together in a family

family: a group of people who care about each other and share their lives together

family counselor: a person who helps a family solve conflict

foster family: when a new set of parents takes care of a child for a while

husband: a man who is married

marriage: when a man and a woman decide to become husband and wife

marriage counselor: a person who helps a husband and wife solve conflict

nuclear family: when a mother, father, and their children live together in a family

single-parent family: when only one parent lives with a family

stepfamily: another word for a blended family

wife: a woman who is married

Index